ROSINSKI - VAN HAMME

THORGAL

The Brand of the Exiles

Colour work: GRAZA

Original title: Thorgal 20 – La marque des bannis

Original edition: © Rosinski & Van Hamme, 1995, Editions du Lombard
(Dargaud-Lombard SA)
www.lelombard.com
All rights reserved

English translation: © 2012 Cinebook Ltd

Translator: Jerome Saincantin
Lettering and text layout: Imadjinn
Printed in Spain by Just Colour Graphic

This edition first published in Great Britain in 2012 by
Cinebook Ltd
56 Beech Avenue
Canterbury, Kent
CT4 7TA
www.cinebook.com

A CIP catalogue record for this book
is available from the British Library

ISBN 978-1-84918-136-5

9th CINEBOOK
The 9th Art Publisher

IT WON'T BE TODAY EITHER, THEN...

THEY SHOULD HAVE BEEN BACK THREE WEEKS AGO. THREE WEEKS!...

IT WAS THEIR LAST EXPEDITION OF THE YEAR. SOON, THE ICE WILL COVER THE SEA.

WHAT WILL BECOME OF US?

I'M SCARED, VIGRID. WHAT WILL WE DO IF OUR MEN DON'T COME BACK? WHO WILL FEED US DURING THE WINTER? WHO WILL PROTECT US FROM RAIDERS AND THE MOUNTAIN TRIBES?

CALM DOWN, ERNHILD. MAYBE THEY JUST WENT A BIT FURTHER THAN THEY HAD INTENDED.

THORGAL OFTEN TOLD ME THAT AS LONG AS ALL THEY CARE ABOUT IS RAIDING AND SENSELESS KILLING, THE VIKINGS WILL NEVER BE A GREAT PEOPLE.

AARICIA, NO...

UNLESS THEY CAME ACROSS THAT DEMON OF THE SEA WE'VE BEEN HEARING ABOUT LATELY. THAT SHAIGAN—THEY SAY HE PILLAGES AND SLAUGHTERS WITHOUT MERCY...

AND WHAT ELSE DO WE DO, IF NOT PILLAGE AND SLAUGHTER WITHOUT MERCY?

IS IT REALLY YOU, GANDALF THE MAD'S DAUGHTER, DARING TO SPEAK THUS?

WHY NOT? ONE CAN BE THE DAUGHTER OF A WARLORD AND STILL BELIEVE IT IS WISER TO BUILD UPON PEACE AT HOME THAN ON FIGHTING ABROAD.

BEWARE, AARICIA! BY SPEAKING IN SUCH A MANNER, YOU DENY THE TEACHINGS OF OUR GODS AND YOU INSULT THE MEMORY OF OUR ANCESTORS. THE VIKINGS ARE THE MASTERS OF THE SEA AND MUST DIE WITH A SWORD IN THEIR HAND IF THEY WANT TO ENTER GREAT ODIN'S VALHALLA.

OH, NO...

I... I CAN'T GO ON. BUT I'M SO CLOSE... IT'S NOT FAIR...

AS FOR YOUR THORGAL, MY LOVELY, ALL HIS PRETTY WORDS DIDN'T STOP HIM FROM ABANDONING YOU ALMOST THREE YEARS AGO. THE TRUTH IS, HE WAS NEVER REALLY ONE OF US. NO DOUBT HE WAS TOO MUCH OF A COWARD TO ACT LIKE A TRUE VIKING.

FORGIVE ME, VIGRID, I... I DON'T KNOW WHAT CAME OVER ME. IT'S JUST THAT WHEN YOU SPOKE OF THORGAL THAT WAY, I....

DON'T TOUCH ME!

WHATEVER MAY HAVE HAPPENED TO OUR HUSBANDS AND OUR SONS, AT LEAST WE CAN SPEAK OF THEM WITHOUT SHAME OR ANGER.

YOU HAD BETTER GO HOME, AARICIA. WE ARE ALL A LITTLE ON EDGE TONIGHT.

THEY'RE GOING TO POUNCE. I... I HAVE TO FIND SHELTER, QUICKLY...

?!?
°°°

THOSE ROCKS, THERE... IF ONLY I COULD REACH THEM...

AAAHH

SAY, JOLAN, WHY DID THORGAL LEAVE?

IT'S... ER... IT'S A LITTLE DIFFICULT TO EXPLAIN...

WHAT'S IT TO YOU, ANYWAY? YOU DON'T EVEN KNOW HIM.

HE'S MY FATHER. AARICIA TOLD ME. SO, I WANT HIM TO COME BACK.

ALL THE OTHER CHILDREN HAVE FATHERS. WHEN THEIR FATHERS GO AWAY, THEY ALWAYS COME BACK WITH NICE PRESENTS AND PRETTY JEWELS. I WISH THORGAL WOULD COME BACK WITH PRESENTS TOO.

AND AARICIA WISHES HE'D COME BACK AS WELL. SHE TOLD ME. SO, WHY ISN'T HE COMING BACK? IS HE MEAN?

OF COURSE NOT. HE'S VERY NICE.

WHY DID HE LEAVE, THEN?

I... I DON'T KNOW, WOLFCUB. STOP ASKING QUESTIONS. I WISH THORGAL WOULD COME BACK TOO.

ARE YOU CRYING? WHY ARE YOU CRYING?

I'M NOT CRYING. COME ON, LET'S GO PLAY OUR GAME.

YAY! I LIKE WHEN YOU MAKE THINGS DISAPPEAR.

BUT, REMEMBER, WOLFCUB: IT'S A SECRET. AARICIA DOESN'T WANT THE GROWNUPS TO KNOW I CAN DO THAT. DO YOU SWEAR?

I SWEAR.

ALL RIGHT. WHAT DO YOU WANT ME TO MAKE DISAPPEAR?

HOW ABOUT THIS STICK HERE?

NO, THAT'S TOO EASY. THAT BIG ROCK, OVER THERE... SIT DOWN, WOLFCUB.

IT WAS TANATLOC*, THORGAL'S FATHER, WHO TAUGHT ME THAT ALL THINGS AND BEINGS IN THE UNIVERSE ARE MADE OF MILLIONS OF TINY STARS LINKED TOGETHER BY ENERGY CURRENTS.

HE TAUGHT ME TO SEE THOSE STARS, AND TO DIRECT THE ENERGY CURRENTS IN ORDER TO CHANGE THE VERY NATURE OF MATTER.

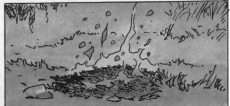

MAKING THINGS DISAPPEAR IS EASY FOR ME NOW. WHAT I HAVE TO MASTER...

... IS RECREATING THEM OR TRANSFORMING THEM. I CAN'T DO THAT YET.

WOOF

WOOF WOOF

WOLFCUB?

WOLFCUB, WHERE ARE YOU? AARICIA TOLD US NOT TO GO TOO FAR FROM THE VILLAGE. WOLFCUB?...

WHAT IS IT, MUFF? EASY, BOY...

GRR GRRR

*SEE THE LAND OF QA.

7

WOLFCUB, ARE YOU ALL RIGHT? ARE YOU HURT

WHAT'S WRONG WITH YOU?! ARE YOU CRAZY? THOSE WOLVES COULD HAVE EATEN YOU!

OF COURSE NOT. THEY'RE MY FRIENDS. I HEARD THEM TALK AMONGST THEMSELVES WHILE YOU WERE MAKING THE STONE DISAPPEAR.

YOU HEARD THEM TALK?!?

YES. THEY TRIED TO CATCH THAT MAN UP THERE ALL NIGHT LONG, AND THEY WERE SAYING IT WOULDN'T BE MUCH LONGER. BUT I TOLD THEM TO LEAVE HIM ALONE.

???

ERIK!...

THAT'S ERIK! THAT'S MY SON! WHAT HAPPENED TO HIM!? WHERE ARE HIS FATHER AND BROTHER!? WHERE ARE THE OTHERS!?

HE'LL TELL US ONCE HE COMES TO. STEP ASIDE, VIGRID. WE'RE BRINGING HIM TO THE LONGHOUSE.

YOU KNOW, I'M THE ONE WHO FOUND HIM. SOME WOLVES WERE ATTACKING HIM, BUT I TOLD THEM TO GO AWAY.

COME IN, EVERYONE. ERIK HAS REGAINED CONSCIOUSNESS! HE'S GOING TO TELL US WHAT HAPPENED.

OUR FOUR DRAKKARS WERE LADEN WITH GOLD AND PLUNDER TAKEN FROM THE SAXONS. OUR LOSSES HAD BEEN LIGHT, AND OUR HEARTS WERE FILLED WITH PRIDE AT THE THOUGHT OF COMING HOME WITH SUCH RICHES...

BUT JUST AS WE ROUNDED THE CAPE OF TWO TIDES, FIVE DAYS' SAIL FROM HERE, A HUGE SHIP, TEN TIMES AS BIG AS THIS HOUSE AND PAINTED ALL IN RED, CAME OUT OF THE MIST AND CUT ACROSS US.

THE BLOOD SHIP OF SHAIGAN THE MERCILESS!

WITH ITS THREE BANKS OF OARS, IT WAS TOO TALL FOR US TO BOARD AND TOO FAST FOR US TO ESCAPE.

WITH SKILFUL MANOEUVRING, IT MANAGED TO SEPARATE OUR DRAKKARS AND ATTACK EACH OF THEM SEPARATELY. WE NEVER HAD A CHANCE TO MOUNT A PROPER DEFENCE.

SHAIGAN HIMSELF WAS AT THE HELM. ALL OF US WERE THUNDERSTRUCK WHEN WE RECOGNISED HIM...

ONE BY ONE, WE WERE OVERWHELMED BY HORDES OF PIRATES, AND MANY OF US DIED HOLDING OUR SWORDS. SO DID MY FATHER AND OLDER BROTHER, WHO PERISHED SCREAMING ODIN'S NAME AT THEIR ENEMIES.

THE SURVIVORS WERE CHAINED AND LOADED ABOARD THE RED SHIP, ALONG WITH OUR PLUNDER AND WEAPONS. THEN, AFTER SETTING FIRE TO OUR DRAKKARS, SHAIGAN SAILED AWAY TO THE SOUTHWEST.

WOUNDED IN THE HEAD AND ARM, I'D BEEN LEFT FOR DEAD. THE HEAT FROM THE FLAMES BROUGHT ME BACK TO MY SENSES, AND I HAD JUST ENOUGH TIME TO JUMP OVERBOARD.

HANGING ONTO A PIECE OF DEBRIS, I DRIFTED FOR A DAY AND A NIGHT UNTIL LUCK SAW ME PICKED UP BY A SMALL FLEET OF VIKINGS FROM THE GREAT FJORD.

THEY TENDED TO MY WOUNDS AND, ONCE ON LAND, LENT ME A HORSE TO COME BACK TO NORTHLAND. BUT THE HORSE DIED ALONG THE WAY, AND I FINISHED THE TRIP ON FOOT.

TELL ME, ERIK: YOU SAID YOU'D RECOGNISED THAT ACCURSED SHAIGAN. WHO IS HE?

WE ALL RECOGNISED HIM. EVEN NOW, I STILL CANNOT BELIEVE WHAT MY EYES SAW, FOR IT WAS ONE OF OUR OWN PEOPLE...

IT WAS THORGAL AEGIRSSON.

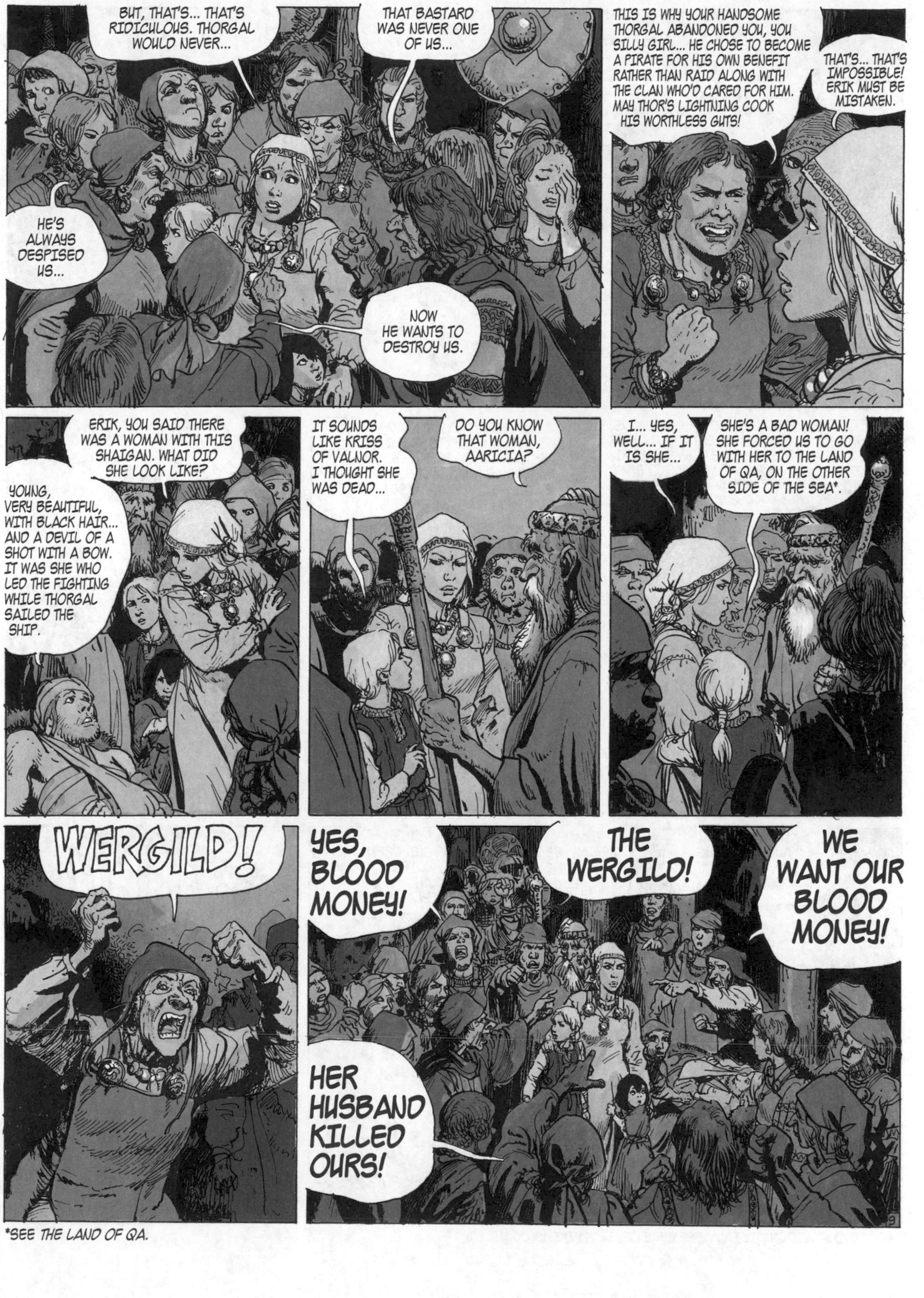
BUT, THAT'S... THAT'S RIDICULOUS. THORGAL WOULD NEVER...
THAT BASTARD WAS NEVER ONE OF US...
HE'S ALWAYS DESPISED US...
NOW HE WANTS TO DESTROY US.
THIS IS WHY YOUR HANDSOME THORGAL ABANDONED YOU, YOU SILLY GIRL... HE CHOSE TO BECOME A PIRATE FOR HIS OWN BENEFIT RATHER THAN RAID ALONG WITH THE CLAN WHO'D CARED FOR HIM. MAY THOR'S LIGHTNING COOK HIS WORTHLESS GUTS!
THAT'S... THAT'S IMPOSSIBLE! ERIK MUST BE MISTAKEN.
ERIK, YOU SAID THERE WAS A WOMAN WITH THIS SHAIGAN. WHAT DID SHE LOOK LIKE?
YOUNG, VERY BEAUTIFUL, WITH BLACK HAIR... AND A DEVIL OF A SHOT WITH A BOW. IT WAS SHE WHO LED THE FIGHTING WHILE THORGAL SAILED THE SHIP.
IT SOUNDS LIKE KRISS OF VALNOR. I THOUGHT SHE WAS DEAD...
DO YOU KNOW THAT WOMAN, AARICIA?
I... YES, WELL... IF IT IS SHE...
SHE'S A BAD WOMAN! SHE FORCED US TO GO WITH HER TO THE LAND OF QA, ON THE OTHER SIDE OF THE SEA*.
WERGILD!
YES, BLOOD MONEY!
THE WERGILD!
WE WANT OUR BLOOD MONEY!
HER HUSBAND KILLED OURS!
9

*SEE *THE LAND OF QA*.

AARICIA, DAUGHTER OF GANDALF, YOU AND YOUR CHILDREN ARE HEREBY SENTENCED TO EXILE, BY THE JUDGEMENT OF THE THING*. YOU WILL LEAVE THE VILLAGE TOMORROW AT DAWN, WITHOUT WEAPONS, FOOD OR MONEY, CARRYING ONLY THE CLOTHES ON YOUR BACK.

YOUR LANDS AND YOUR HUSBAND'S, YOUR JEWELLERY AND ALL YOUR POSSESSIONS WILL BE DISTRIBUTED AS WERGILD TO THOSE WOMEN AMONG US WHOSE HUSBANDS AND SONS DID NOT COME BACK.

NO ONE ON VIKING LANDS WILL BE ALLOWED TO OFFER YOU ASSISTANCE, ON PAIN OF BEING EXILED AS WELL. AND, SO THAT EVERYONE CAN RECOGNISE YOU FOR WHAT YOU HAVE BECOME...

YOU SHALL BEAR ON YOUR FACE THE MARK OF THE EXILED!

NO...

KILL ME IF YOU WANT, BUT I BEG YOU, NOT THAT... NOT THAT!...

I AM SORRY, AARICIA, BUT IT IS THE LAW. BE GLAD THAT YOUR CHILDREN WILL BE SPARED THE BRANDING BECAUSE OF THEIR YOUTH. EXECUTE THE SENTENCE!

AAAAAHHHH

*GOVERNING AND JUDICIAL ASSEMBLY OF EACH VIKING CLAN

12

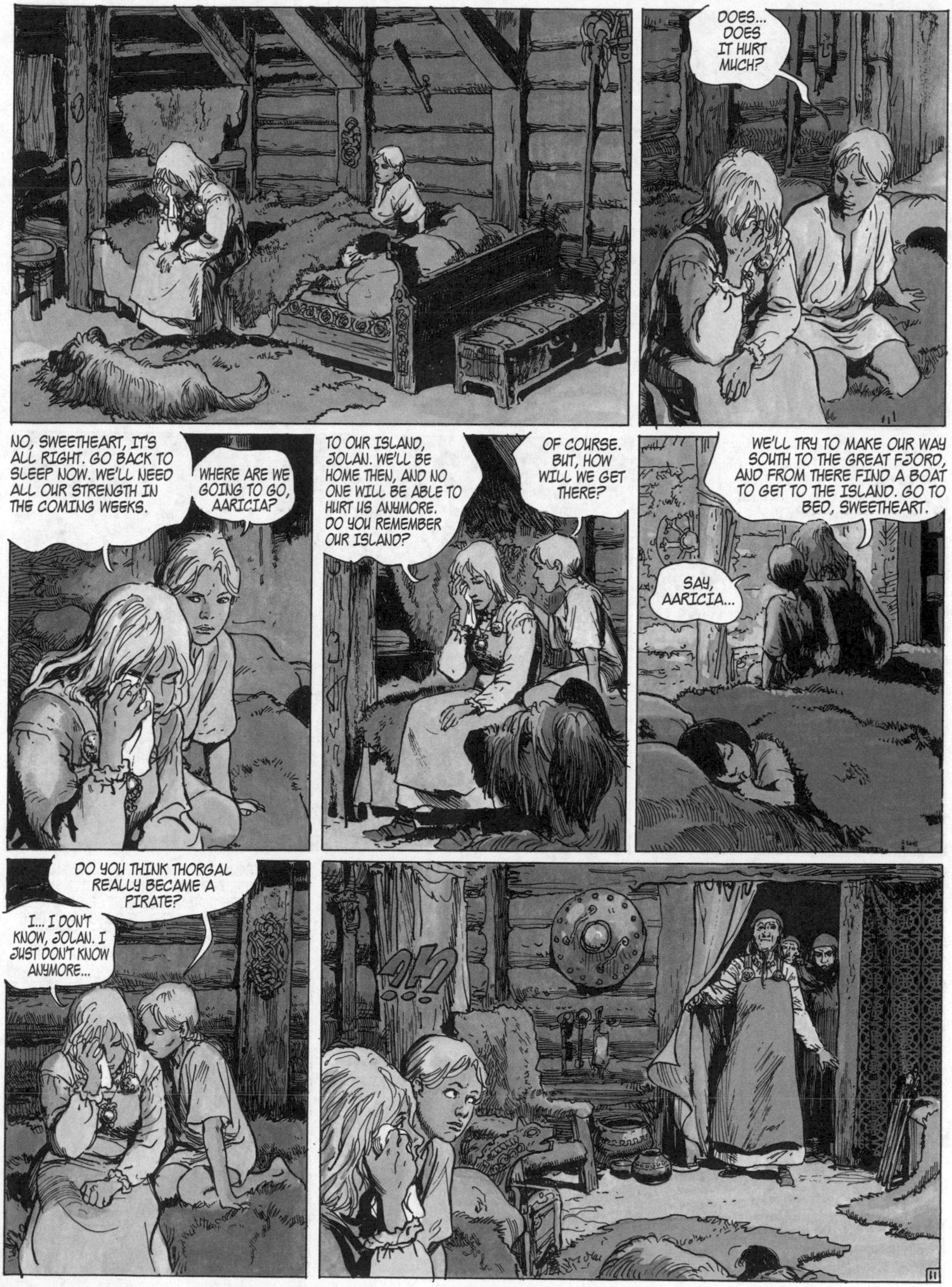
DOES... DOES IT HURT MUCH?
NO, SWEETHEART, IT'S ALL RIGHT. GO BACK TO SLEEP NOW. WE'LL NEED ALL OUR STRENGTH IN THE COMING WEEKS.
WHERE ARE WE GOING TO GO, AARICIA?
TO OUR ISLAND, JOLAN. WE'LL BE HOME THEN, AND NO ONE WILL BE ABLE TO HURT US ANYMORE. DO YOU REMEMBER OUR ISLAND?
OF COURSE. BUT, HOW WILL WE GET THERE?
WE'LL TRY TO MAKE OUR WAY SOUTH TO THE GREAT FJORD, AND FROM THERE FIND A BOAT TO GET TO THE ISLAND. GO TO BED, SWEETHEART.
SAY, AARICIA...
DO YOU THINK THORGAL REALLY BECAME A PIRATE?
I... I DON'T KNOW, JOLAN. I JUST DON'T KNOW ANYMORE...

WHAT ARE YOU DOING HERE? YOU HAVE NO RIGHT! I'M NOT SUPPOSED TO LEAVE THE VILLAGE UNTIL DAWN.

SO, WE SHOULD GIVE YOU TIME TO HIDE YOUR GOLD AND JEWELS? I DON'T THINK SO, MY PRETTY!

AND, FOR STARTERS, GIVE ME THAT! IT'LL BARELY BE ENOUGH TO PAY ME BACK FOR THE LOSS OF A HUSBAND AND SON.

OW!

GO ON, ALL OF YOU! EMPTY THE CHESTS; SEARCH THE COFFERS. MAKE THAT WENCH GIVE US BACK ALL THAT HER THIEF OF A FATHER STOLE FROM US WHEN HE CALLED HIMSELF OUR KING!

EVIL HAGS! I'M GOING TO...

NO, JOLÁN!

I KNOW WHAT YOU ARE CAPABLE OF, BUT WE CANNOT DO ANYTHING TO THEM. IF YOU HURT THEM, ALL THREE OF US WILL BE KILLED.

WELL, "PRINCESS"? NOT SO HIGH AND MIGHTY ANYMORE, ARE YOU? YOU'RE NOTHING, NOW! YOU'RE LESS THAN THE POOREST OF BEGGARS, LESS THAN THE MANGIEST OF DOGS! FARE THEE WELL, "PRINCESS"! I CHERISH THE THOUGHT THAT YOUR CORPSE WILL SOON FEED THE CROWS!

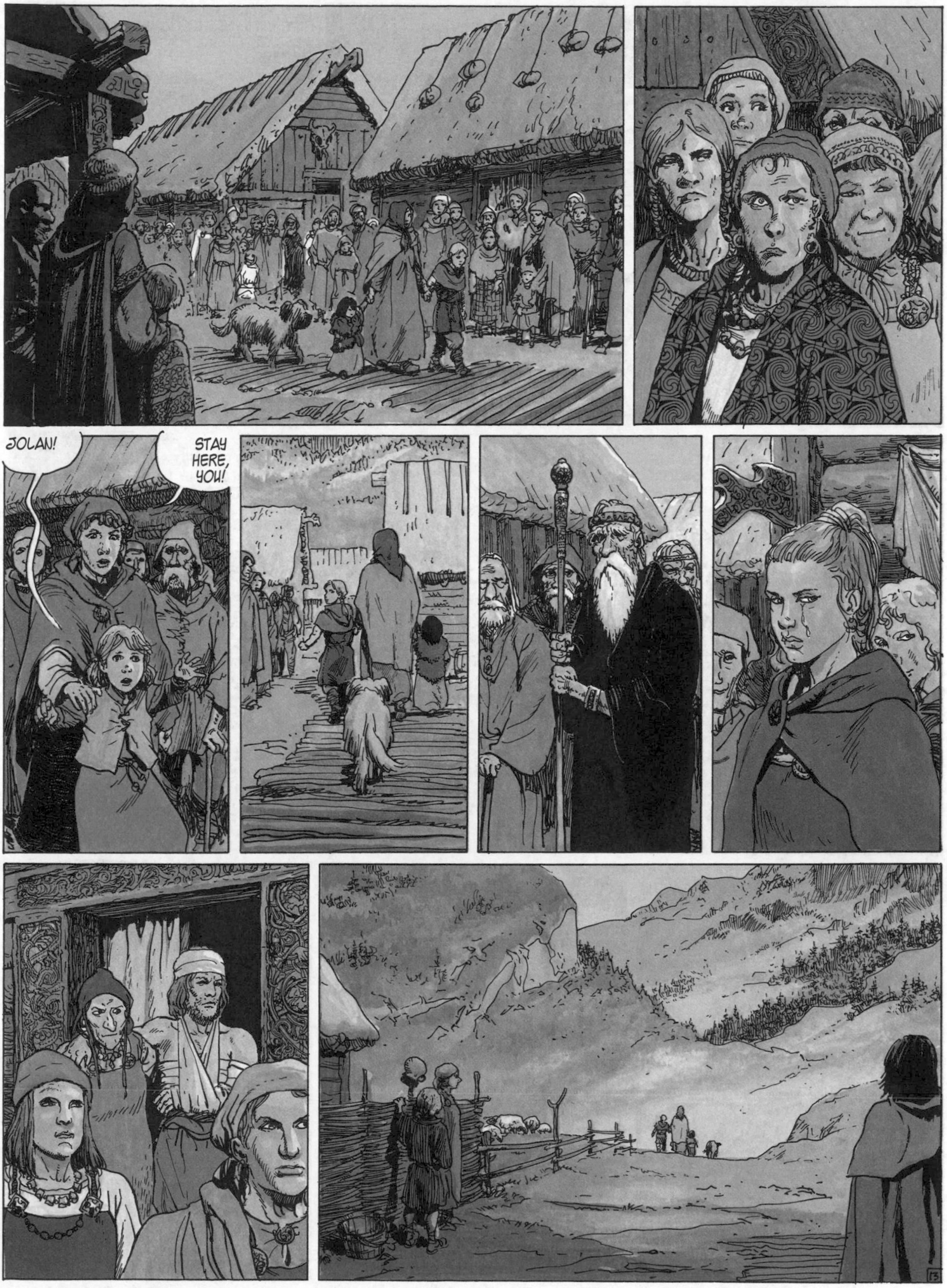
JOLAN!
STAY HERE, YOU!

THEN WE'LL FIND ROOTS, PINE NUTS, ACORNS... AND WE'LL TRY TO CATCH A RABBIT...

PSSSST, AARICIA...

MAMA, I'M HUNGRY.

WE'LL STOP SOON, SWEETHEART, AND WE'LL GATHER SOME FRUITS AND WILD BERRIES.

THERE AREN'T ANY BERRIES ANYMORE, AARICIA. IT'S THE BEGINNING OF WINTER.

SOLVEIG?! ARE YOU CRAZY!? WHAT ARE YOU DOING HERE?

NO ONE SAW ME LEAVE THE VILLAGE. I WAS VERY CAREFUL. COME THIS WAY.

I BROUGHT YOU THIS HORSE AND SLED WITH SOME FURS AND FOOD FOR THREE WEEKS. DON'T WORRY... IT'S ALL MINE. NO ONE WILL KNOW I GAVE IT TO YOU. ONCE YOU REACH THE GREAT FJORD, YOU CAN EXCHANGE THE HORSE FOR A BOAT.

I ALSO BROUGHT YOU YOUR KNIFE, A SALVE FOR YOUR BURN, AND A FEW ITEMS OF JEWELLERY YOU CAN SELL IF YOU NEED TO.

OH, SOLVEIG, YOU'RE SAVING OUR LIVES! BUT YOU'RE TAKING A TERRIBLE RISK...

IF ANYONE DISCOVERS WHAT YOU DID, YOU'LL BE EXILED TOO.

WOULDN'T YOU HAVE DONE THE SAME THING? YOU'RE MY ONLY FRIEND, AARICIA. IF I COULD, I'D LEAVE WITH YOU.

FAREWELL, MY PRINCESS! I HOPE YOU GET BACK TO YOUR ISLAND AND FIND A PEACEFUL LIFE THERE.

FAREWELL, SOLVEIG! I'LL NEVER FORGET YOU.

WHY DON'T WE BUILD A FIRE, AARICIA? IT WOULD WARM US UP AND KEEP WILD ANIMALS AWAY.

A FIRE CAN BE SEEN FROM A LONG WAY AWAY AT NIGHT, JOLAN. IN OUR CIRCUMSTANCES, MEN ARE A MUCH BIGGER THREAT THAN ANIMALS.

WE'RE EXILES, MY POOR BOY. AMONG VIKINGS, IT MEANS THAT ANYONE CAN STEAL FROM US, ENSLAVE US OR EVEN KILL US, WITHOUT ANYONE BEING ABLE TO HELP US IN ANY WAY.

THIS IS ALL THORGAL'S FAULT. I... I HATE HIM.

YOU HATE HIM TOO, DON'T YOU?

NO, I DON'T HATE HIM. I'M JUST TRYING TO UNDERSTAND.

OH, THAT'S EASY...

THORGAL LEFT TO GO LIVE WITH ANOTHER WOMAN. SEVERAL MEN IN THE VILLAGE HAVE DONE THE SAME. AND KRISS OF VALNOR CONVINCED HIM TO BECOME A PIRATE WITH HER, THAT'S ALL.

IS THAT REALLY ALL?...

YOU'RE FORGETTING THAT THORGAL ONLY EVER WANTED TO FIGHT TO DEFEND HIS LIFE AND OURS. HE HATED GRATUITOUS VIOLENCE. AND, ABOVE ALL... HE LOVED US.

WELL, HE DOESN'T LOVE US ANYMORE. HE EVEN CHANGED HIS NAME, AND BECAUSE OF HIM WE WERE DRIVEN OUT OF THE VILLAGE AND THEY PUT THAT... THAT MARK ON YOUR CHEEK. I HATE HIM!

CALM DOWN, SWEETHEART. WE'RE NOT EVEN SURE IT WAS REALLY HE. IT'S LIKELY THAT SHAIGAN SIMPLY LOOKS LIKE HIM. GO TO SLEEP NOW. WE'LL LEAVE VERY EARLY TOMORROW.

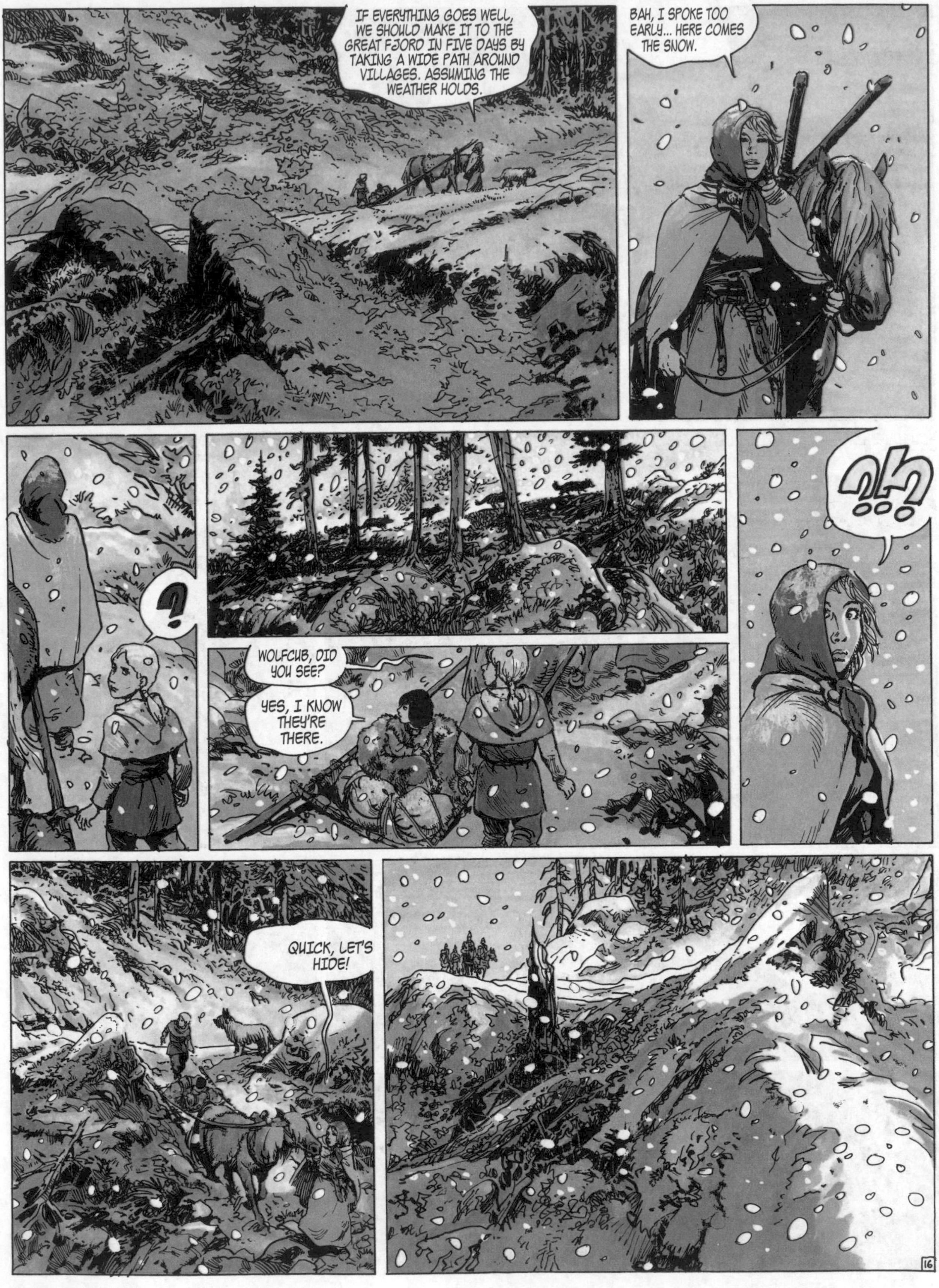
IF EVERYTHING GOES WELL, WE SHOULD MAKE IT TO THE GREAT FJORD IN FIVE DAYS BY TAKING A WIDE PATH AROUND VILLAGES. ASSUMING THE WEATHER HOLDS.
BAH, I SPOKE TOO EARLY... HERE COMES THE SNOW.
?
WOLFCUB, DID YOU SEE?
YES, I KNOW THEY'RE THERE.
?!!?
QUICK, LET'S HIDE!
16

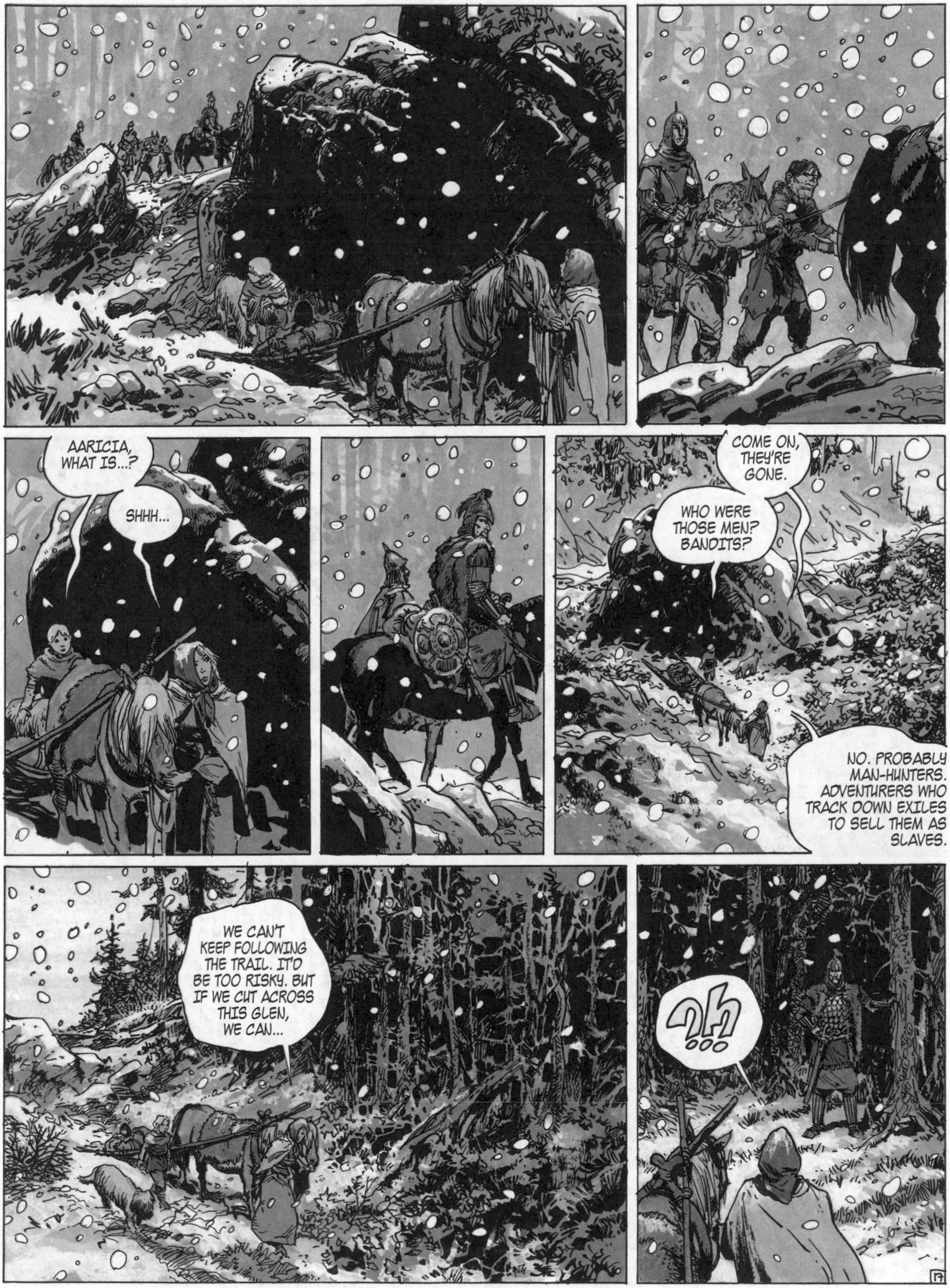
AARICIA, WHAT IS...?
SHHH...
COME ON, THEY'RE GONE.
WHO WERE THOSE MEN? BANDITS?
NO. PROBABLY MAN-HUNTERS. ADVENTURERS WHO TRACK DOWN EXILES TO SELL THEM AS SLAVES.
WE CAN'T KEEP FOLLOWING THE TRAIL. IT'D BE TOO RISKY. BUT IF WE CUT ACROSS THIS GLEN, WE CAN...
AH...
17

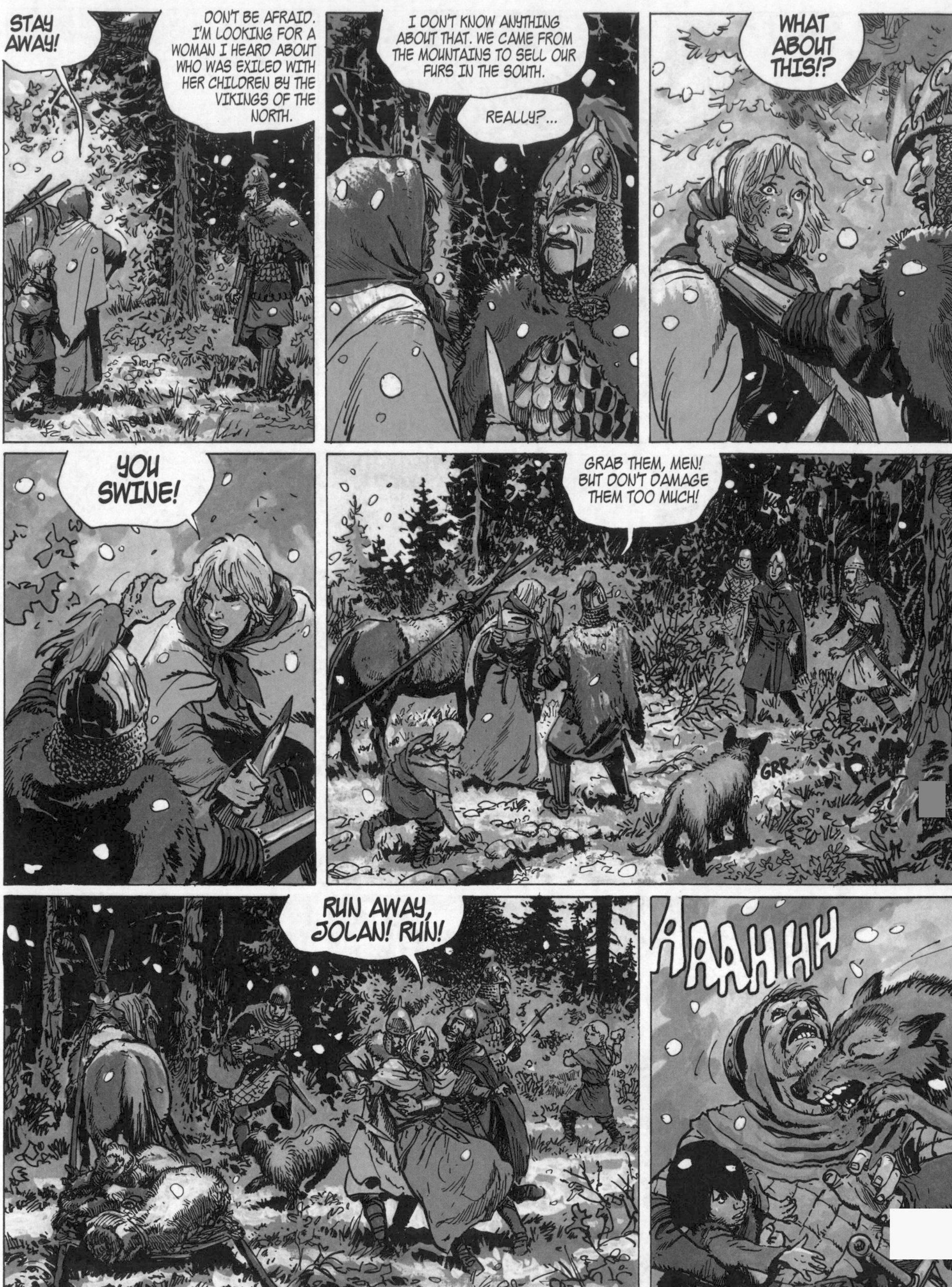
STAY AWAY!
DON'T BE AFRAID. I'M LOOKING FOR A WOMAN I HEARD ABOUT WHO WAS EXILED WITH HER CHILDREN BY THE VIKINGS OF THE NORTH.
I DON'T KNOW ANYTHING ABOUT THAT. WE CAME FROM THE MOUNTAINS TO SELL OUR FURS IN THE SOUTH.
REALLY?...
WHAT ABOUT THIS!?
YOU SWINE!
GRAB THEM, MEN! BUT DON'T DAMAGE THEM TOO MUCH!
GRR
RUN AWAY, JOLAN! RUN!
¡AAHHH
18

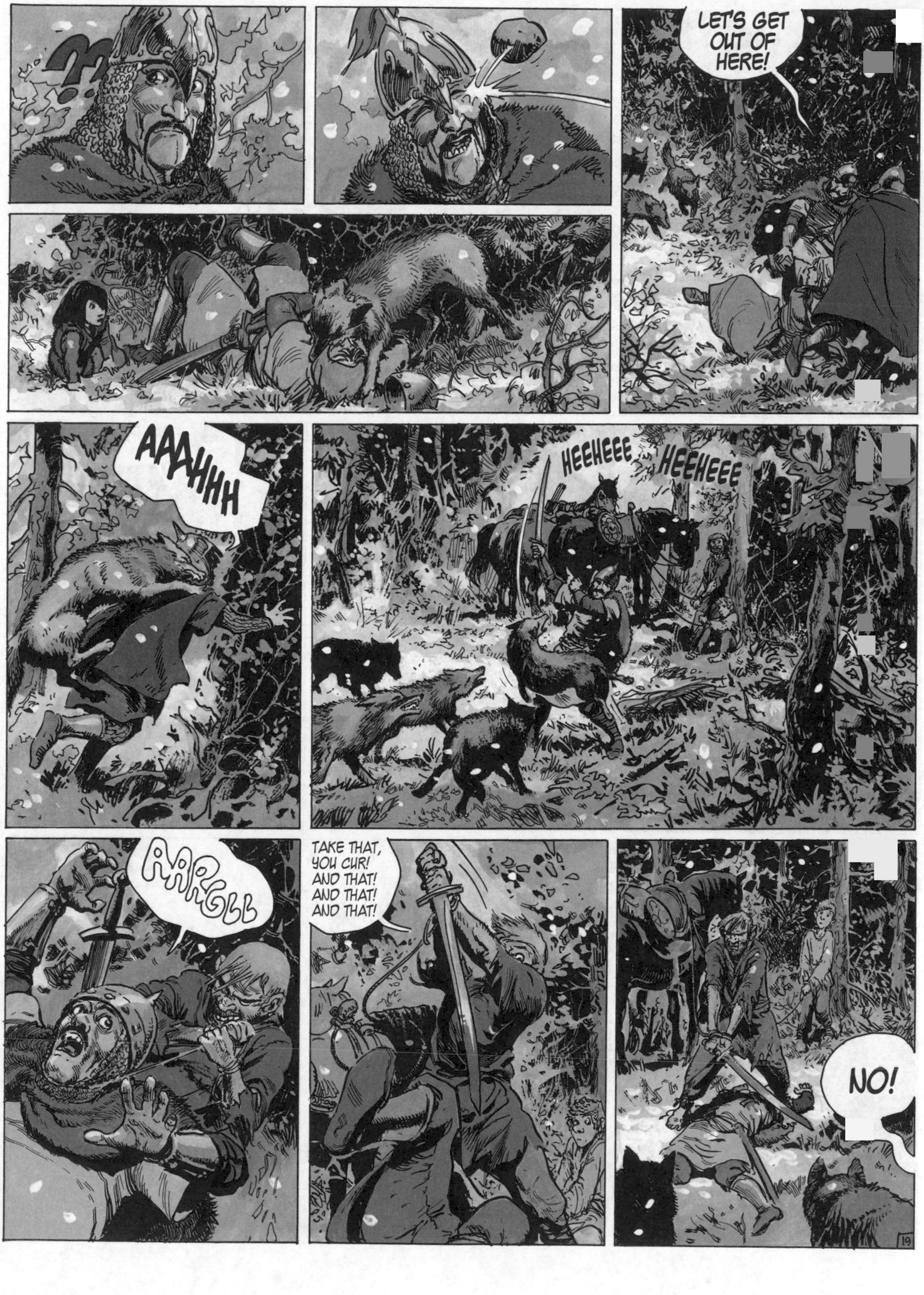
LET'S GET OUT OF HERE!
AAAHHH
HEEHEEE
HEEHEEE
AARGLL
TAKE THAT, YOU CUR! AND THAT! AND THAT! AND THAT!
NO!
19

DON'T WORRY. THEY WON'T HURT YOU IF YOU'RE NICE TO THEM. THEY'RE MY FRIENDS.

??

YOUR DAUGHTER HAS SOME SURPRISING PROTECTORS, WOMAN. YOU'LL NEED THEM, FOR I SEE THAT YOU, TOO, BEAR THE MARK OF THE EXILES.

NEVER YOU MIND.

AT LEAST THOSE PIGS HAVE FINALLY PAID FOR THEIR CRIMES. BUT, WHERE'S THEIR LEADER?

THAT WAY. I KNOCKED HIM OUT AND LEFT MY DOG TO WATCH HIM.

MUFF!?!

22

THE MAN WHO ESCAPED IS CALLED ARKADES. HE WORKS FOR A BIG SLAVER OF THE GREAT FJORD, A BYZANTINE WHO BUYS PRISONERS OR CAPTURES EXILES TO SELL THEM BEYOND THE SEA.

GOING SOUTH IS DANGEROUS. YOU SHOULD COME HIDE IN THE MOUNTAINS WITH ME. IT'S THE ONLY WAY FOR EXILES LIKE US TO SURVIVE.

YOU CAN GO WHERE YOU WISH. I'M STOPPING HERE FOR THE NIGHT. WE'VE HAD MORE THAN OUR SHARE OF EXCITEMENT, AND THE CHILDREN ARE TIRED.

HOW'S YOUR DOG?

HE'S GOT A DEEP CUT ON HIS SIDE, BUT IT DIDN'T GO PAST THE MUSCLE.

MY PARENTS WERE KILLED TWO YEARS AGO. THAT ONE... I DON'T EVEN KNOW HIS NAME. HE WAS ALREADY THEIR PRISONER WHEN THEY CAPTURED ME.

MY NAME'S DAREK. WHAT'S YOURS?

JOLAN. IS THAT MAN YOUR FATHER?

I DON'T LIKE THAT MAN, AARICIA. HE LOOKS LIKE A BANDIT, AND HE ATE HALF THE FOOD WE HAD LEFT.

SHHH... TOMORROW, HE'LL GO HIS OWN WAY. SLEEP, SWEETHEART.

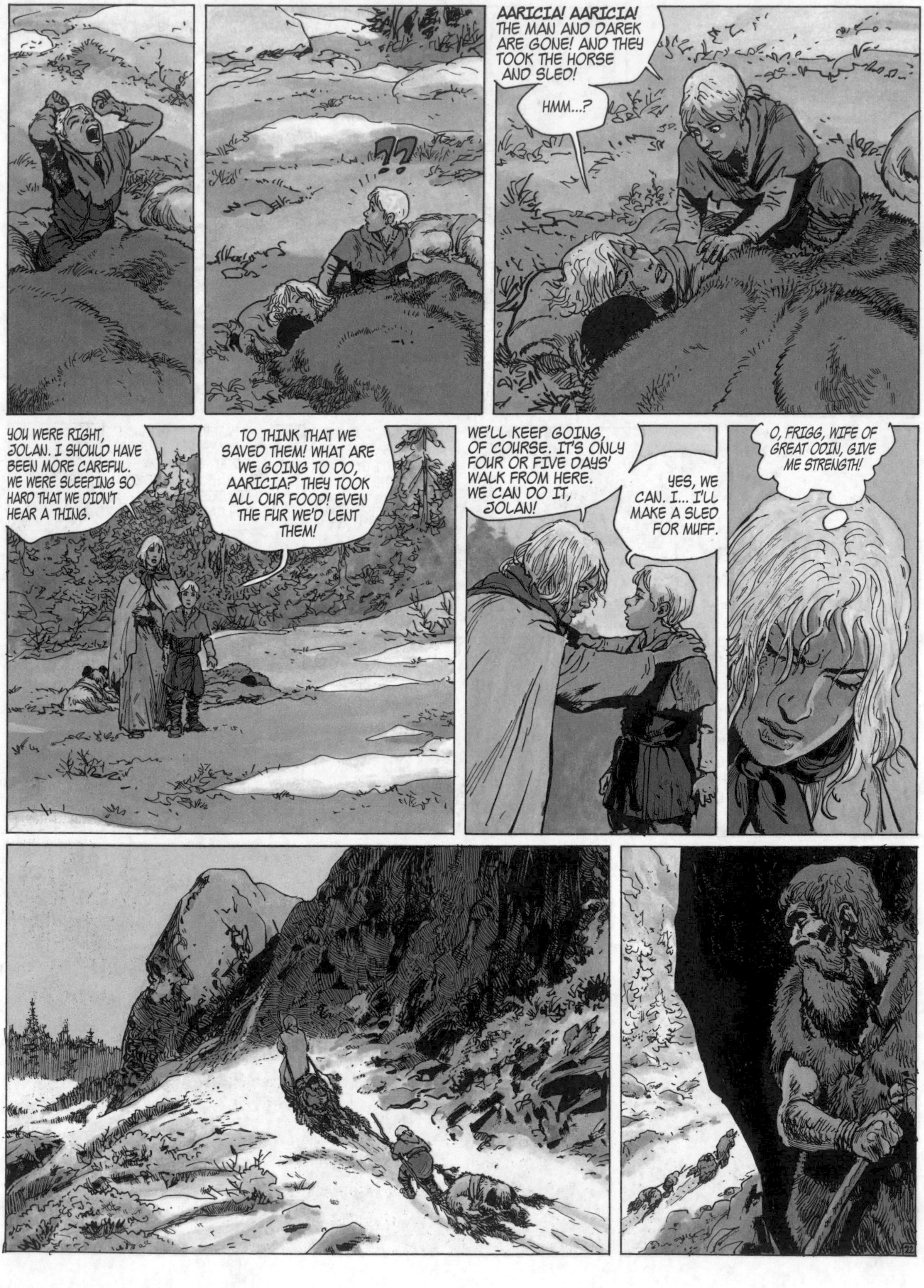
AARICIA! AARICIA! THE MAN AND DAREK ARE GONE! AND THEY TOOK THE HORSE AND SLED!
HMM...?
YOU WERE RIGHT, JOLAN. I SHOULD HAVE BEEN MORE CAREFUL. WE WERE SLEEPING SO HARD THAT WE DIDN'T HEAR A THING.
TO THINK THAT WE SAVED THEM! WHAT ARE WE GOING TO DO, AARICIA? THEY TOOK ALL OUR FOOD! EVEN THE FUR WE'D LENT THEM!
WE'LL KEEP GOING, OF COURSE. IT'S ONLY FOUR OR FIVE DAYS' WALK FROM HERE. WE CAN DO IT, JOLAN!
YES, WE CAN. I... I'LL MAKE A SLED FOR MUFF.
O, FRIGG, WIFE OF GREAT ODIN, GIVE ME STRENGTH!

A WOMAN AND TWO CHILDREN. IT'LL BE EASY.

NO.

LOOK AT THOSE WOLVES... THEY'RE NOT ATTACKING. IT LOOKS LIKE THEY'RE PROTECTING THEM.

WHAT MAGIC IS THIS?...

I DON'T KNOW, BUT I DON'T WANT TO RISK THE WRATH OF THE WOLF-GOD. BESIDES, THAT WOMAN CAN'T HAVE MUCH WORTH STEALING.

DON'T LOOK AT ME LIKE THAT, JOLAN. THIS HORRIBLE MARK...

LATER, WHEN I'M OLDER, I'LL MAKE IT DISAPPEAR.

I KNOW I'LL BE ABLE TO DO IT. TANATLOC TAUGHT ME HOW TO. BUT I HAVE TO WAIT UNTIL I CAN REMAKE THINGS. I'M STILL TOO YOUNG TO DO THAT.

A SON WITH STRANGE POWERS... A DAUGHTER WHO CAN SPEAK WITH THE WOLVES SHE'S NAMED AFTER... SUCH PECULIAR CHILDREN THORGAL GAVE ME!...

OH, MY DARLINGS... MY DARLINGS... YOU'RE ALL I HAVE LEFT IN THE WORLD!...

AH, IT SEEMS TO BE ABATING AT LAST...

MAMA, LOOK!

THE WOLVES... THEY'RE GOING!

IF THEY'RE LEAVING US, IT CAN MEAN ONLY ONE THING...

THE GREAT SOUTHERN FJORD!

WHAT DO YOU WANT, KID?

I... I'D LIKE TO BUY A BOAT.

IS THAT SO? AREN'T YOU A LITTLE YOUNG TO GO OUT TO SEA?

IT'S... IT'S FOR MY FATHER. HE'S SICK, AND HE TOLD ME TO COME HERE IN HIS STEAD TO FIND A BOAT SO WE CAN KEEP TRAVELLING.

HMM... AND WITH WHAT WOULD HE PAY FOR THAT BOAT, YOUR FATHER?

WITH MY MOTHER'S JEWELS. HERE, I BROUGHT THIS ONE. IT'S GOLD.

YEAH, NOT BAD. BUT OUR WOMEN HAVE ENOUGH JEWELLERY AS IT IS, MY BOY. AND WE NEED OUR BOATS TO GO FISHING.

YOU SHOULD ORDER ONE FROM THE CARPENTER INSTEAD. WITH ANY LUCK, YOU'LL HAVE IT IN TWO OR THREE MONTHS— WHEN THE FJORD'S ICEBOUND! HA! HA! HA!

PSSSST... JOLAN... ARE YOU LOOKING FOR A BOAT?

IF YOU HAVE OTHER NECKLACES LIKE THIS ONE, I MIGHT BE ABLE TO GET YOU ONE.

DAREK!?!

MAMA, I'M SO HUNGRY...

JOLAN WILL SOON BE BACK WITH SOME FOOD, SWEETHEART. AT LEAST, I HOPE SO.

THIEVES! SCAMPS! MY CHICKENS! COME BACK HERE!

IT'SH NOT RIGHT TO SHTEAL...

WE'RE CHILDREN OF EXILES, JOLAN. STEALING IS THE ONLY WAY FOR US TO SURVIVE. HOW DO YOU THINK I GOT THESE CLOTHES?

THAT'S WHY WE LEFT WITH YOUR HORSE AND FOOD THE OTHER DAY. I KNOW—I SHOULD BE ASHAMED. ESPECIALLY AFTER WHAT YOU'D DONE FOR US. BUT, IN OUR SITUATION... YOU'LL SEE. IT'S EVERY MAN FOR HIMSELF.

I THINK WE CAN BE STRONGER TOGETHER THAN ALONE.

MAYBE. I DON'T KNOW. WE DIDN'T HELP OURSELVES MUCH BY STEALING FROM YOU. SHORTLY AFTER WE LEFT YOU, WE WERE ATTACKED BY MEN FROM A MOUNTAIN TRIBE WHO WANTED TO TAKE THE HORSE FROM US. I MANAGED TO RUN AWAY AND MAKE MY WAY HERE, THOUGH.

WHEN YOU TOLD ME ABOUT FINDING A BOAT FOR US, I SUPPOSE YOU INTENDED TO STEAL IT, TOO?

OF COURSE. HOW ELSE COULD I GET MY HANDS ON A BOAT? COME ON... LET'S BRING THESE CHICKENS TO YOUR MOTHER AND LITTLE SISTER, PREFERABLY WHILE STAYING OUT OF SIGHT.

MAMA! THERE'S A RIDER APPROACHING!

?!!

QUICK! LET'S GO HIDE IN THE FOREST!

28

AARICIA! WAIT... IT'S ME, ERIK...

ERIK!? BUT, HOW?...

SOLVEIG TOLD ME YOU WANTED TO GET TO THE GREAT FJORD, AND I TRIED TO CATCH UP TO YOU. YOU CANNOT STAY HERE, AARICIA. YOU'RE IN DANGER.

I'M IN DANGER EVERYWHERE, ERIK. THANKS TO YOU.

I... I'M SO ASHAMED... IT WAS YOUR CHILDREN WHO SAVED ME FROM THE WOLVES, AND I... AS SOON AS I COULD STAND UP, I TOLD SOLVEIG EVERYTHING AND JUMPED ON A HORSE TO FOLLOW YOUR TRAIL AND COME WARN YOU...

WARN ME OF WHAT?

I... I LIED, AARICIA. IN PART, ANYWAY.

WHEN YOU SAID THAT SHAIGAN WAS ACTUALLY THORGAL?

BUT, THAT VERY EVENING, THE BLACK-HAIRED WOMAN OFFERED ME A DEAL. SHE'D LET ME GO SO I COULD TELL WHAT I'D SEEN, ON THE CONDITION THAT I WOULDN'T SAY I'D BEEN CAPTURED AND SHE'D SPOKEN TO ME. WHY DID SHE CHOOSE ME? PROBABLY BECAUSE I WAS THE YOUNGEST OF THE SURVIVORS AND MY WOUNDS WERE MINOR.

NO, IT REALLY WAS THORGAL. WE ALL RECOGNISED HIM. I LIED WHEN I SAID THAT I'D BEEN LEFT FOR DEAD ON MY BURNING DRAKKAR. THE TRUTH IS THAT I WAS TAKEN CAPTIVE LIKE ALL THE OTHER SURVIVORS.

AT THE TIME, I DIDN'T SEE WHAT COULD BE WRONG WITH ACCEPTING. I SWORE, AND SHE HAD ME DROPPED ON THE COAST A FEW DAYS' WALK FROM OUR VILLAGE. SO, I WASN'T PICKED UP BY THE VIKINGS OF THE GREAT FJORD LIKE I SAID.

BUT WHY? TO WHAT END, ALL OF THAT?

IT SHOULDN'T BE HARD TO UNDERSTAND, MY DEAR...

... BUT IT'LL BE MY PLEASURE TO EXPLAIN IT TO YOU PERSONALLY.

KRISS OF VALNOR!?!

29

I'M A SVEAR* FROM THE EASTERN SEA, ON THE OTHER SIDE OF THE MOUNTAINS. MY FATHER WAS EXILED FOR KILLING THE SON OF OUR CLAN CHIEF IN A DUEL, AND HE WAS FORCED TO RUN FROM THE LAND WITH MY MOTHER, MY SISTER AND ME.

THE CHIEF SENT SOME MEN AFTER US, AND MY PARENTS WERE MASSACRED WITHOUT HAVING A CHANCE TO DEFEND THEMSELVES. MY FATHER HAD JUST ENOUGH TIME TO HIDE MY SISTER AND ME IN A CAVE BEFORE THEY CAUGHT UP TO HIM. THAT WAS TWO YEARS AGO.

SINCE THEN, WE'VE LIVED LIKE WILDERMEN IN THE MOUNTAINS, STEALING WHAT WE NEED FROM VILLAGES. BUT, A FEW WEEKS AGO, MY SISTER WAS CAPTURED BY THE MEN OF THAT ACCURSED BYZANTINE SLAVER.

AND YOU DIDN'T GET CAUGHT?

I'D GONE TO CATCH TROUT IN A NEARBY STREAM. AS YOU SAW, THOUGH, THEY EVENTUALLY GOT ME, TOO. AND, IF IT HADN'T BEEN FOR YOU...

HERE WE ARE. AARICIA?... IT'S ME, JOLAN. I'M WITH DAREK, AND WE BROUGHT SOME FOOD.

AARICIA?... WOLFCUB?... THEY'RE GONE. SOMETHING MUST HAVE HAPPENED...

AND NOT SOMETHING GOOD. LOOK: THE SNOW IS ALL TRAMPLED.

MUFF! WHAT HAPPENED? WHERE ARE AARICIA AND WOLFCUB?

*ANCIENT SWEDES

30

THAT'S ERIK, THE MAN FROM OUR VILLAGE WHO CAUSED US TO BE EXILED. I DON'T UNDERSTAND...

WHAT I UNDERSTAND IS THAT YOUR MOTHER AND SISTER ARE IN SERIOUS TROUBLE.

MOST LIKELY, THE BYZANTINE'S MEN TRACKED THEM DOWN. THERE'S NOTHING WE CAN DO.

YES, THERE IS! WE CAN GO FREE THEM. AND YOUR SISTER, TOO, WHILE WE'RE AT IT.

YOU THINK I NEVER CONSIDERED IT?... IT'S IMPOSSIBLE, JOLAN. THE BYZANTINE HAS A WHOLE GANG OF HIS COUNTRYMEN WITH HIM, WHILE THERE ARE JUST TWO OF US—TWO CHILDREN WITH ONLY A CHICKEN-SPIT FOR A WEAPON.

WHERE'S YOUR BYZANTINE HIDING?

IN A STONE KEEP HALF A DAY'S WALK FROM HERE. A REAL FORTRESS. HE KEEPS HIS SLAVES THERE UNTIL HE CAN SHIP THEM OUT IN THE SPRING. IT'S HOPELESS, JOLAN.

LET'S GO!

HERE WE ARE. BE CAREFUL—THERE'RE BOUND TO BE SOME SENTRIES.

I'M TELLING YOU THERE'S NO POINT.

WE'LL SEE WHEN WE GET THERE.

31

WHAT?... THOSE MEN ARE VIKINGS!?!

VIKINGS OF THE NORTH, YES.

THEY'LL MAKE STRONG SLAVES THAT YOU'LL BE ABLE TO SELL FOR A HIGH PRICE IN YOUR COUNTRY.

THAT'S... THAT'S MADNESS!! WE'RE IN VIKING LAND HERE! IF THE PEOPLE OF THE GREAT FJORD WERE TO HEAR OF IT...

WHY SHOULD THEY? ALL YOU HAVE TO DO IS MAKE SURE THAT NONE OF YOUR PRISONERS ESCAPES. WHY DON'T WE SETTLE OUR BUSINESS NOW?...

HERE'S THE SUM WE AGREED UPON. WILL YOU DO ME THE HONOUR OF SHARING MY MEAL?

I DON'T THINK SO.

TOO RARELY DO I ENJOY THE PLEASURE OF HAVING A GUEST AS RADIANT AS YOU, KRISS OF VALNOR. I WAS HOPING...

HOPE IS THE LOSER'S PREROGATIVE, BYZANTINE. A CATEGORY YOU WILL INEVITABLY BELONG TO, SHOULD YOU DECIDE TO HARASS THE WIFE OF SHAIGAN THE MERCILESS.

YOU WILL HAVE FOOD FOR TWO BROUGHT TO MY ROOM. I WILL SAIL AT DAWN WITH MY PRISONER.

ARENT YOU HUNGRY, MY DEAR? A PITY: THIS RABBIT STEW IS DELICIOUS. HOW LONG HAS IT BEEN SINCE YOU AND THE KID ATE ANYTHING?

I'M TELLING YOU TO EAT! I WANT YOU HEALTHY AND STRONG TO SERVE ME.

YOU ACCURSED WITCH! YOU'LL PAY FOR ALL YOUR CRIMES!

AND WHO WILL MAKE ME PAY FOR THEM, YOU FOOL!? NOT YOUR BELOVED THORGAL, THAT'S FOR CERTAIN...

BECAUSE OUR BRAVE HERO HAS COMPLETELY LOST HIS MEMORY! HE DOES WHAT I WANT HIM TO, AND HE DOESN'T EVEN REMEMBER THAT YOU EXIST!

MAMA!...

YOU WILL BE MY PERSONAL SLAVE, AARICIA. I'LL HAVE YOUR HEAD SHAVED SO EVERYONE CAN SEE THE MARK OF YOUR ENSLAVEMENT. AND YOUR DAUGHTER'S LIFE WILL GUARANTEE YOUR OBEDIENCE.

I WAS SURE THAT ONCE THEY LEARNT WHO SHAIGAN THE MERCILESS WAS, YOUR PEOPLE WOULD EXILE YOU IN RETALIATION. JUST AS I WAS SURE THAT YOU'D HEAD FOR THE GREAT FJORD TO FIND A WAY TO SAIL TO YOUR ISLAND. SO, I ASKED THE BYZANTINE TO CAPTURE YOU, BUT THAT IDIOT FAILED MISERABLY. FORTUNATELY, AS YOU CAN SEE, I GOT HERE IN TIME TO GIVE YOU A PROPER WELCOME.

YOU REALLY SHOULD EAT, MY PRETTY. AT THIS POINT, THE ONLY THING YOU HAVE LEFT TO LOSE IS YOUR LIFE.

THE MAIN ENTRANCE IS TOO WELL GUARDED. WE'LL HAVE TO ENTER THE KEEP FROM THE BACK.

THE BACK?!?...

BUT, THE BACK OVERLOOKS THE SEA! ANYWAY, WHY WOULD I BE CRAZY ENOUGH TO WANT TO ENTER THAT KEEP? THERE ARE AT LEAST 20 GUARDS INSIDE.

YOU CAN REMAIN HERE WITH MUFF, DAREK. BUT I'M GOING.

YOU STAY HERE, MUFF. I'LL BE BACK SOON.

THIS KID'S INSANE... WHY ARE YOU SO STUBBORN ABOUT THIS, JOLAN? ALL WE'RE GOING TO GET OUT OF IT IS THAT WE'LL JOIN THE OTHERS AS SLAVES!

BECAUSE THORGAL WOULD HAVE DONE IT!

THORGAL? WHO'S THAT?...

MY... SOMEONE WHO TAUGHT ME THAT YOU SHOULD NEVER GIVE UP. FIND YOURSELF A LOG TO HANG ONTO AND LET'S GO!

I... I.... I'M... F... FR... FREEZING. I S... JUST L.. LOVE SW... SW... SWIMMING IN WIN.. WINTER.

M... ME T... TOO. B... B... BUT THIS S... S... SNOW IS A G... GODS-SEND F... FOR US.

34

ABSOLUTELY. THAT WAY THEY WON'T FIND OUR CORPSES UNTIL SPRING. WHAT DO WE DO NOW?

WE NEED TO REACH THAT WINDOW UP THERE.

I SHOULD BE ABLE TO. CLIMBING IS MY THING.

THEN, GO AHEAD! YOU'RE BOUND TO FIND A ROPE YOU CAN THROW DOWN TO ME. BE CAREFUL: THESE STONES MUST BE HORRIBLY SLIPPERY WITH THE SNOW.

WITH THOSE VIKINGS, WE HAVE A FULL SHIPMENT. MAYBE WE SHOULD TRY TO MAKE ONE LAST TRIP.

THAT WOULD SAVE US HAVING TO FEED THEM FOR MONTHS—AND GIVE US A CHANCE TO SPEND WINTER HOME, AWAY FROM THIS ICY LAND.

THAT WOULD BE WONDERFUL, MY LORD.

WE'LL TALK ABOUT IT AGAIN TOMORROW MORNING. BEFORE YOU TURN IN, GO SEE IF EVERYTHING'S IN ORDER DOWNSTAIRS AND IF THE GUARDS ARE AT THEIR POSTS.

AS YOU COMMAND. GOOD NIGHT, MY LORD.

AHHH... I WAS ALMOST DEAD. WHERE DO YOU THINK THE PRISONERS ARE KEPT?

IN THE CELLARS, AS ALWAYS. THE BYZANTINE JUST SENT ARKADES DOWN THERE.

JOLAN, I... I'M SCARED.

SO AM I. THE BEST THING TO DO IN THAT CASE IS TO PRETEND YOU'RE NOT. PICK A WEAPON AND LET'S GO!

TINKLE

PHEWWW... THAT WAS STUPID! WE ALMOST GOT CAUGHT.

I'D FORGOTTEN I HAD THAT NECKLACE IN MY BELT. LET'S HEAD FURTHER DOWN BEFORE HE COMES BACK.

36

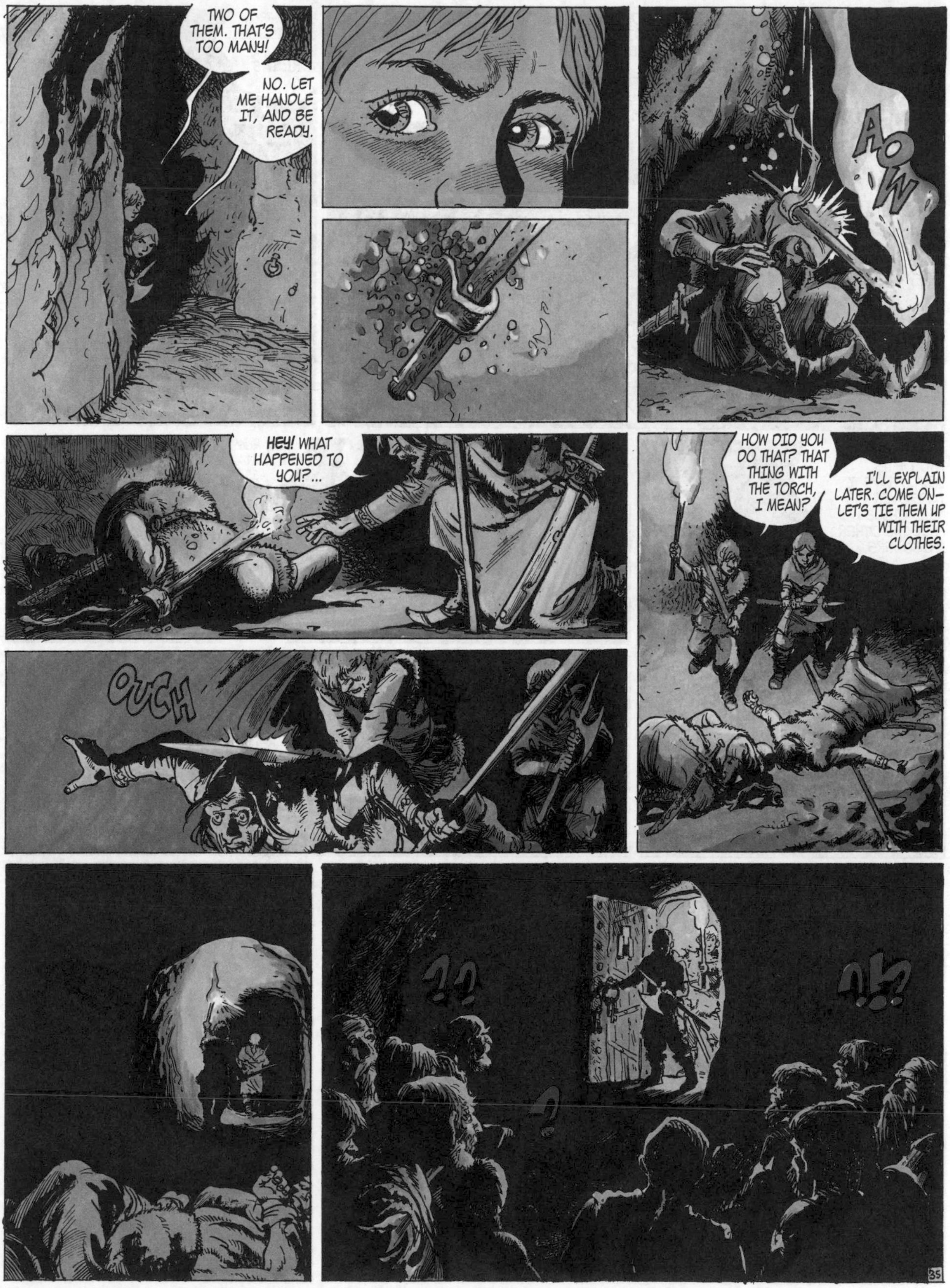
TWO OF THEM. THAT'S TOO MANY!
NO. LET ME HANDLE IT, AND BE READY.
AOW
HEY! WHAT HAPPENED TO YOU?...
HOW DID YOU DO THAT? THAT THING WITH THE TORCH, I MEAN?
I'LL EXPLAIN LATER. COME ON— LET'S TIE THEM UP WITH THEIR CLOTHES.
OUCH
?!?
35

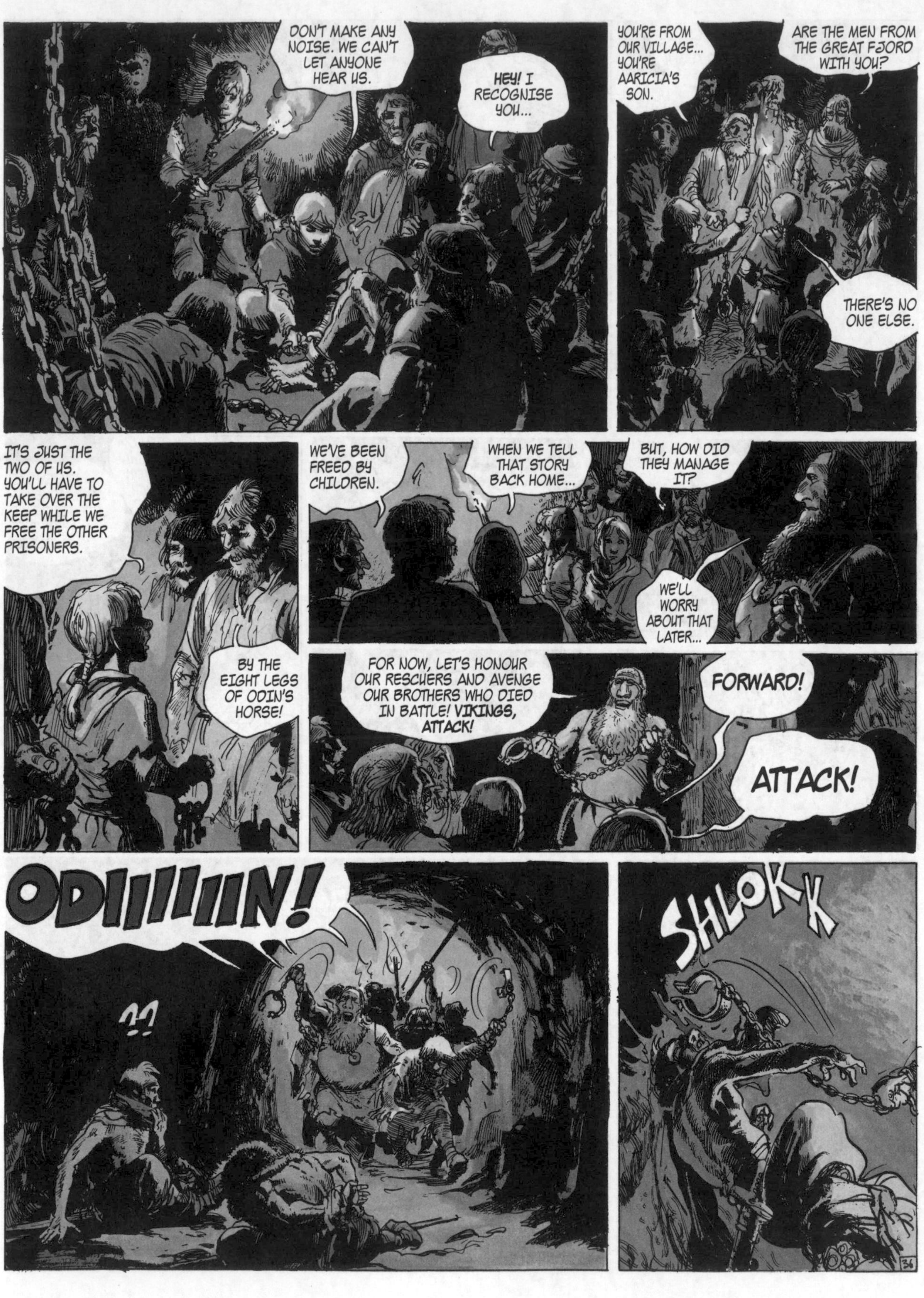

DON'T MAKE ANY NOISE. WE CAN'T LET ANYONE HEAR US.
HEY! I RECOGNISE YOU...
YOU'RE FROM OUR VILLAGE... YOU'RE AARICIA'S SON.
ARE THE MEN FROM THE GREAT FJORD WITH YOU?
THERE'S NO ONE ELSE.
IT'S JUST THE TWO OF US. YOU'LL HAVE TO TAKE OVER THE KEEP WHILE WE FREE THE OTHER PRISONERS.
BY THE EIGHT LEGS OF ODIN'S HORSE!
WE'VE BEEN FREED BY CHILDREN.
WHEN WE TELL THAT STORY BACK HOME...
BUT, HOW DID THEY MANAGE IT?
WE'LL WORRY ABOUT THAT LATER...
FOR NOW, LET'S HONOUR OUR RESCUERS AND AVENGE OUR BROTHERS WHO DIED IN BATTLE! VIKINGS, ATTACK!
FORWARD!
ATTACK!
ODIIIIIIN!
??
SHLOKK
36

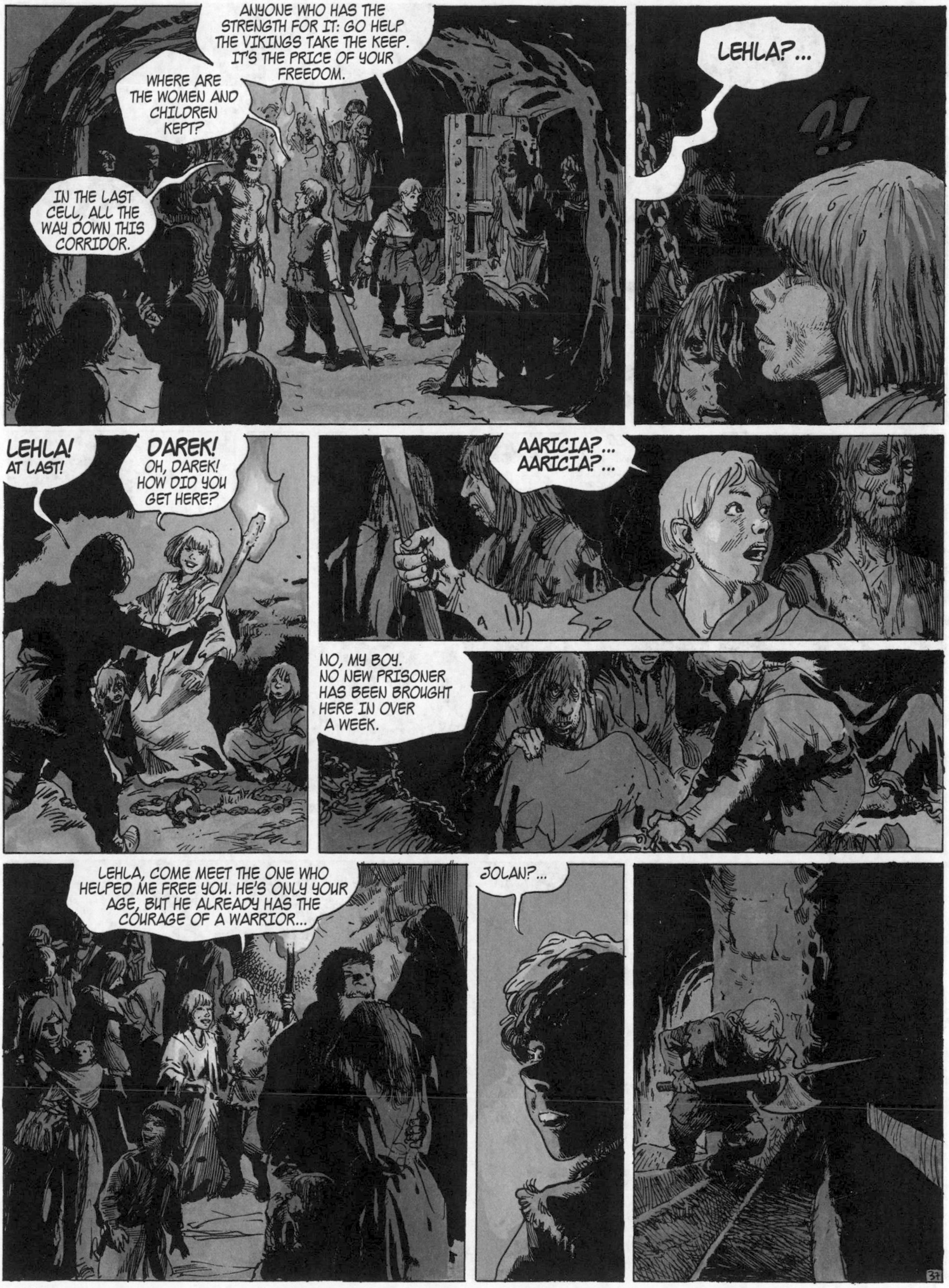
ANYONE WHO HAS THE STRENGTH FOR IT: GO HELP THE VIKINGS TAKE THE KEEP. IT'S THE PRICE OF YOUR FREEDOM.
WHERE ARE THE WOMEN AND CHILDREN KEPT?
IN THE LAST CELL, ALL THE WAY DOWN THIS CORRIDOR.
LEHLA?...
?!
LEHLA! AT LAST!
DAREK! OH, DAREK! HOW DID YOU GET HERE?
AARICIA?... AARICIA?...
NO, MY BOY. NO NEW PRISONER HAS BEEN BROUGHT HERE IN OVER A WEEK.
LEHLA, COME MEET THE ONE WHO HELPED ME FREE YOU. HE'S ONLY YOUR AGE, BUT HE ALREADY HAS THE COURAGE OF A WARRIOR...
JOLAN?...

A FAIR-HAIRED PRISONER AND HER LITTLE GIRL ARRIVED HERE TODAY. WHERE ARE THEY?!

THE... THE TOWER CHAMBER...

THANKS!

OUCHH

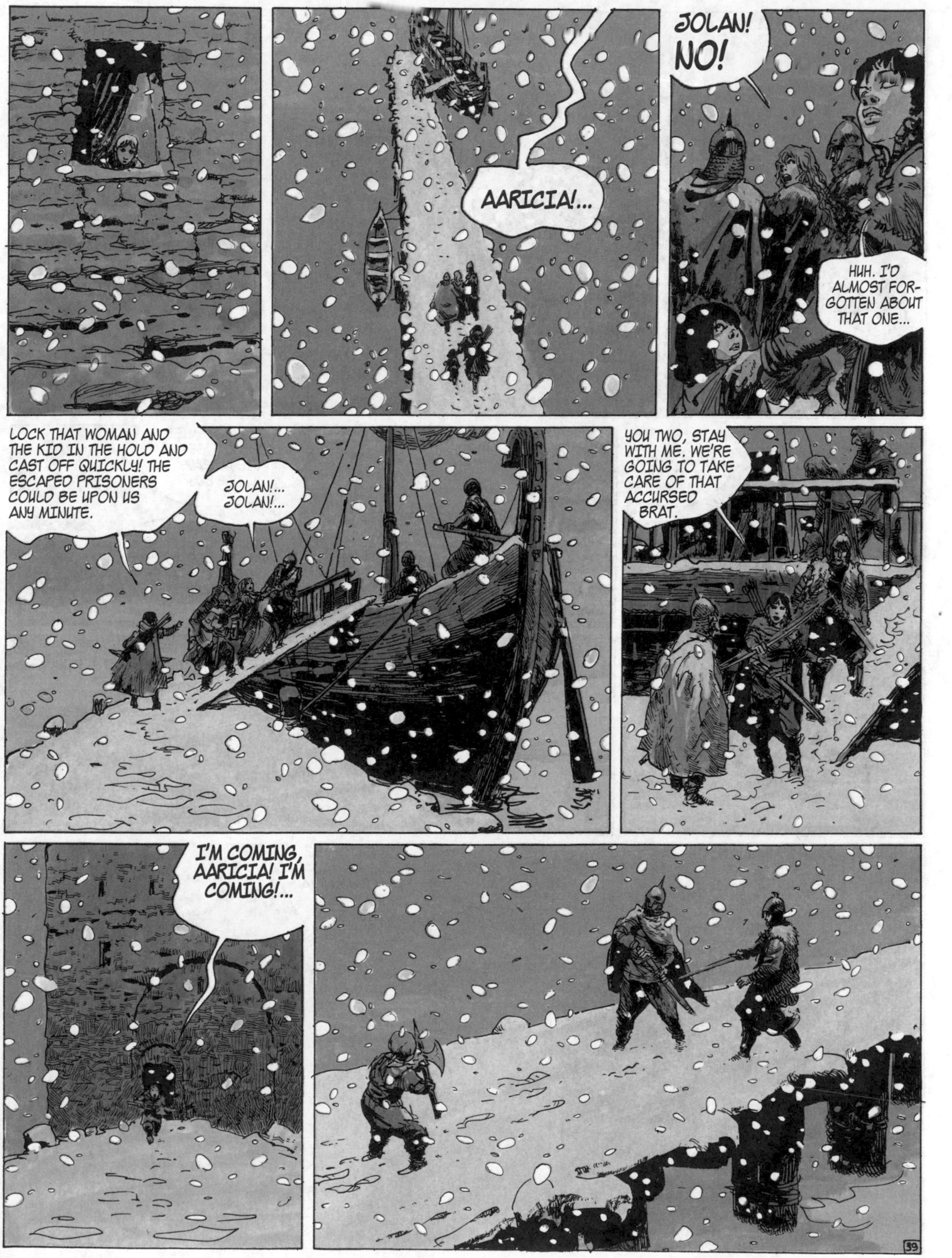
AARICIA!...
JOLAN! NO!
HUH. I'D ALMOST FORGOTTEN ABOUT THAT ONE...
LOCK THAT WOMAN AND THE KID IN THE HOLD AND CAST OFF QUICKLY! THE ESCAPED PRISONERS COULD BE UPON US ANY MINUTE.
JOLAN!... JOLAN!...
YOU TWO, STAY WITH ME. WE'RE GOING TO TAKE CARE OF THAT ACCURSED BRAT.
I'M COMING, AARICIA! I'M COMING!...
39

IMPRESSIVE, JOLAN. YOUR FATHER HIMSELF COULDN'T HAVE DONE BETTER.

BUT, I WON'T MISS. ARE YOU EAGER TO DIE ALREADY, LITTLE BOY?

I WANT YOU TO GIVE ME BACK AARICIA AND WOLFCUB, KRISS OF VALNOR. HAVE YOU FORGOTTEN WHAT YOU OWE ME?

THERE SHE IS!

SHE'S GETTING AWAY!

GET HER!

I NEVER FORGET ANYTHING, JOLAN. WHICH IS WHY YOU'RE STILL ALIVE. I'M AFRAID WE HAVE TO CUT THIS CONVERSATION SHORT, THOUGH...

YOUR MOTHER AND SISTER BELONG TO ME NOW. JUST LIKE YOUR FATHER. IF YOU WANT TO SEE THEM AGAIN, YOU'LL HAVE TO COME GET THEM...

... BUT I DOUBT YOU'LL FIND THAT EASY! HA! HA! HA! GOODBYE, LITTLE BOY!

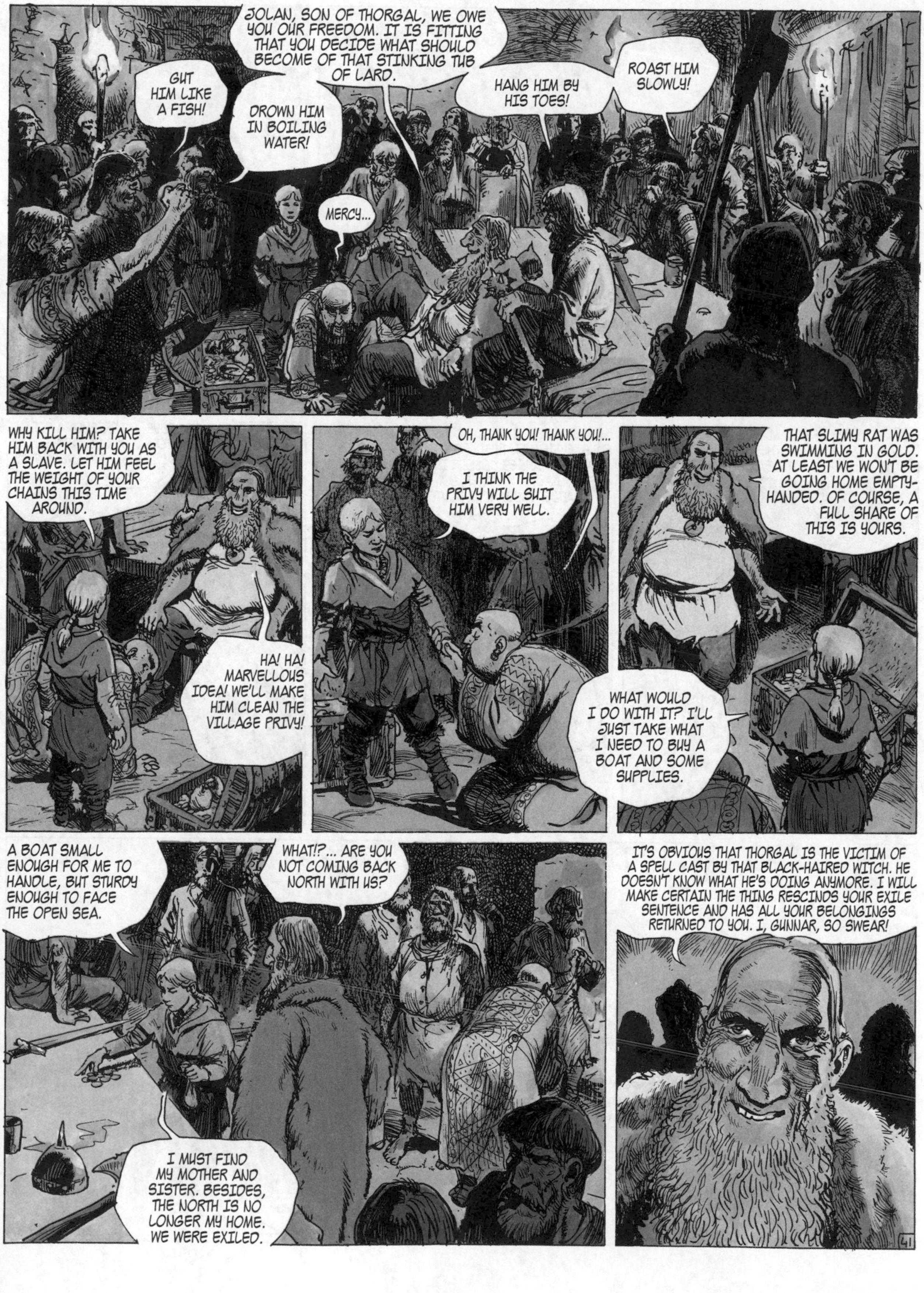

JOLAN, SON OF THORGAL, WE OWE YOU OUR FREEDOM. IT IS FITTING THAT YOU DECIDE WHAT SHOULD BECOME OF THAT STINKING TUB OF LARD.
GUT HIM LIKE A FISH!
DROWN HIM IN BOILING WATER!
HANG HIM BY HIS TOES!
ROAST HIM SLOWLY!
MERCY...
WHY KILL HIM? TAKE HIM BACK WITH YOU AS A SLAVE. LET HIM FEEL THE WEIGHT OF YOUR CHAINS THIS TIME AROUND.
HA! HA! MARVELLOUS IDEA! WE'LL MAKE HIM CLEAN THE VILLAGE PRIVY!
OH, THANK YOU! THANK YOU!...
I THINK THE PRIVY WILL SUIT HIM VERY WELL.
THAT SLIMY RAT WAS SWIMMING IN GOLD. AT LEAST WE WON'T BE GOING HOME EMPTY-HANDED. OF COURSE, A FULL SHARE OF THIS IS YOURS.
WHAT WOULD I DO WITH IT? I'LL JUST TAKE WHAT I NEED TO BUY A BOAT AND SOME SUPPLIES.
A BOAT SMALL ENOUGH FOR ME TO HANDLE, BUT STURDY ENOUGH TO FACE THE OPEN SEA.
WHAT!?... ARE YOU NOT COMING BACK NORTH WITH US?
I MUST FIND MY MOTHER AND SISTER. BESIDES, THE NORTH IS NO LONGER MY HOME. WE WERE EXILED.
IT'S OBVIOUS THAT THORGAL IS THE VICTIM OF A SPELL CAST BY THAT BLACK-HAIRED WITCH. HE DOESN'T KNOW WHAT HE'S DOING ANYMORE. I WILL MAKE CERTAIN THE THING RESCINDS YOUR EXILE SENTENCE AND HAS ALL YOUR BELONGINGS RETURNED TO YOU. I, GUNNAR, SO SWEAR!
41

ARE YOU CERTAIN YOU WILL NOT CHANGE YOUR MIND? WE OWE YOU A DEBT. HOW CAN WE REPAY IT?

BY TAKING THESE EXILES WITH YOU.

ACCEPT THEM INTO THE VILLAGE, AND GIVE THEM LAND SO THEY CAN RECOVER THEIR DIGNITY AS FREE MEN. YOUR CLAN WILL BE THE RICHER FOR THEIR PRESENCE AND THEIR TOIL.

HMM... A MOST UNUSUAL REQUEST. BUT, I PROMISE YOU I WILL ASK THE THING TO LOOK FAVOURABLY UPON IT.

HERE. IF YOU MUST SAIL OUT TO SEA, THEN TAKE THIS, AT LEAST.

WHAT IS IT?

A VIKING'S MOST PRECIOUS POSSESSION AFTER HIS SWORD: A **SUNSTONE!**

IF YOU HOLD IT AT RIGHT ANGLES TO THE SUN'S RAYS, EVEN WHEN THEY ARE HIDDEN BY CLOUDS OR FOG, IT CHANGES COLOUR INSTANTLY. THAT WAY, EVEN IN BAD WEATHER, YOU WILL ALWAYS BE ABLE TO SET YOUR ROUTE BY THE SUN*.

THANK YOU, GUNNAR. THIS IS A PRICELESS GIFT.

*CORDIERITE (A CYCLOSILICATE) AND ICELAND SPAR (A CALCITE) ARE TWO MINERALS FOUND IN SCANDINAVIA THAT HAVE THIS PECULIAR PROPERTY. IT HAS BEEN THEORISED THAT THE VIKINGS USED THEM TO SAIL THE OPEN SEAS.

GOODBYE, MY FRIEND! A PITY WE HAVE TO GO OUR SEPARATE WAYS ALREADY. WE MADE A GOOD TEAM!

TO EVERY MAN HIS FATE, DAREK. MAYBE OURS WILL LEAD US TO CROSS PATHS AGAIN SOMEDAY.

GOOD LUCK, JOLAN! AND THANK YOU.

42

44

WELL, WE'RE TOGETHER AGAIN, MUFF. JUST YOU AND ME. TONIGHT, WE SAIL...

I DON'T KNOW WHERE, OR HOW, BUT WE'LL FIND THEM. I PROMISE YOU THAT: WE'LL FIND THEM.

THAT NECKLACE BELONGS TO YOU, I BELIEVE. IT'S TIME WE SETTLED OUR ACCOUNTS, YOU LITTLE TOAD!

ARKADES!?

I LOST EVERYTHING BECAUSE OF YOU: MY MEN, MY MASTER AND MY DREAMS OF WEALTH AND FORTUNE. YOU WILL PAY FOR ALL OF THAT.

K... KILLING ME WON'T CHANGE WHAT HAPPENED...

GRRR...

NO, BUT IT'LL MAKE ME FEEL BETTER!

45

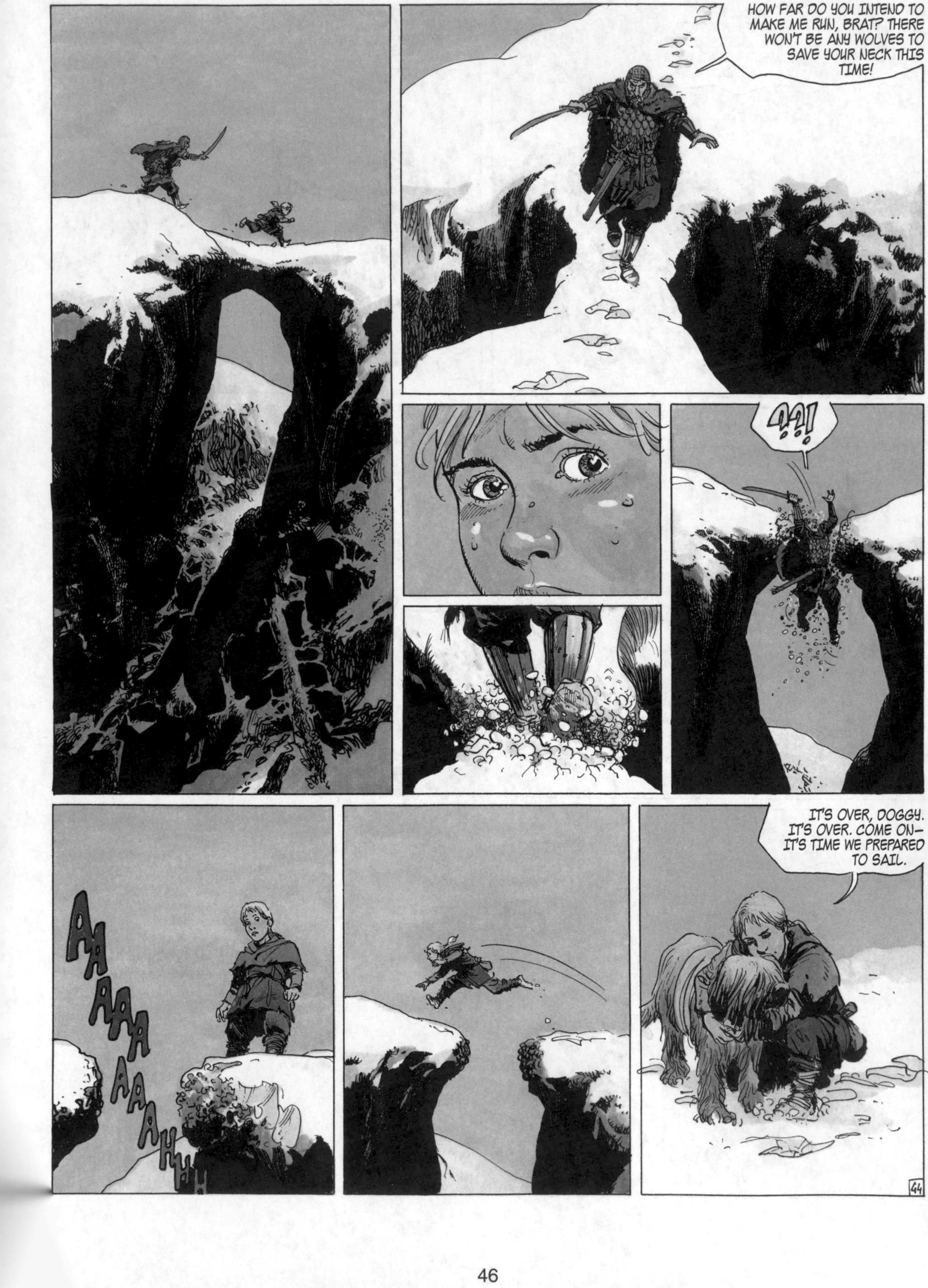
HOW FAR DO YOU INTEND TO MAKE ME RUN, BRAT? THERE WON'T BE ANY WOLVES TO SAVE YOUR NECK THIS TIME!
?!?!
AAAAAAAAHHH
IT'S OVER, DOGGY. IT'S OVER. COME ON– IT'S TIME WE PREPARED TO SAIL.
44

FOR THE GOLD YOU GAVE US, YOU HAVE THE BEST BOAT ON THE ENTIRE COAST, MY BOY. PLUS, WE PACKED ENOUGH FOOD AND WATER FOR TWO MONTHS. BUT, DO YOU REALLY INTEND TO SAIL ALONE?

I HAVE NO CHOICE. I'LL BE ALL RIGHT.

WELL, IT'S YOUR BUSINESS, AFTER ALL. DO BE CAREFUL, THOUGH. WINTER STORMS CAN BE DEADLY.

HO, CAPTAIN!...

DID YOU MEAN TO LEAVE WITH-OUT A CREW?

DAREK?! BUT, I THOUGHT...

BAH! AS WE SAY BACK HOME: ONLY MENHIRS NEVER CHANGE THEIR MIND.

IN THE END, THE THOUGHT OF WINDING UP STUCK IN A NORTHERN VILLAGE DIDN'T SOUND TOO EXCITING. WE HAVE NO FAMILY, NO COUNTRY, JOLAN. SO, WHY NOT GO WITH YOU?

IT'S JUST... ER...

WASN'T IT YOU WHO SAID THAT WE COULD BE STRONGER TOGETHER? I... BORROWED SOME CLOTHES FOR MY LITTLE SISTER, AND HERE WE ARE!

IF YOU'LL HAVE US, OF COURSE.

DO YOU KNOW WHERE YOUR MOTHER AND SISTER ARE?

THEY WERE TAKEN BY KRISS OF VALNOR, THE ACCOMPLICE OF SHAIGAN THE MERCILESS.

THE... THE PIRATE!?

THEY SAY HE SAILS ON A SHIP PAINTED WITH THE BLOOD OF HIS VICTIMS.

YOU'RE RIGHT: IT'S TOO DANGEROUS. LET ME GO ALONE.

MAYBE HE'LL LET US JOIN HIS CREW... I'VE ALWAYS DREAMT OF BEING A PIRATE. DO YOU KNOW WHERE WE CAN FIND THIS SHAIGAN?

SOMEWHERE TO THE SOUTHWEST. BUT, THE SEA IS WIDE...

GOOD! FINDING HIM WILL BE EVEN MORE REWARDING. TAKE THE HELM, CAPTAIN, AND TAKE US SOUTHWEST.

THE END

48